T0199129

English or Amerikish

"Appalachian/Tennessee style"

Pamalamadingdong

To order additional copies of this book, contact:
Xlibris
1-888-795-4274
www.Xlibris.com
Orders@Xlibris.com

ISBN: Softcover   978-1-9845-8502-8
         EBook   978-1-9845-8501-1

Print information available on the last page

Rev. date: 08/04/2020

ENGLISH OR AMERIKISH

(Appalachian/Tennessee Style)
By
Pamalamadingdong

My name is "Pamalamadingdong" I am English and I live in North East Tennessee.

On one of my trips back to England to visit my family I was taking my grandson, Nigel, who was six at the time to school. He had visited me and his Granddad "Hopalong" here twice.

I was stopped at the red light on the dual carriageway, which is called the highway in America and he said,

"Did you know I can count to ten in Turkish Nan,'cos Dad is Turkish?" he said. He proceeded to do so. I asked him what he called his Turkish Nan? He told me "l call her Babanne and Granddad is Dede." "Oh", I replied, "I've learned something new today, thanks Nigel."

As the lights changed to green I heard him say, "l reckon I can speak Amerikish Nan." I laughed, but his little face in the rear view mirror was so serious and I thought about it for a moment. Well, of course to a six year old the languages are English, Spanish, Polish, Danish, Swedish and Turkish, so you bet it was going to be Amerikish!

This little incident impacted me so much that it inspired me to write this story to educate kids throughout the world about the differences in English and Amerikish (Appalachian/Tennessee style), and what's more IT'S TRUE!

Bless you Nigel! Here we go..............

1.

Sophie, Zak and Nigel came on a big plane across the ocean from Manchester, England with their Mummies to Tennessee in the United States of America.

Alice is Sofie and Zak's Mum and Susan is Nigel's Mum.

Sophie is 7 years old, Zak is 5 and Nigel is 6.

All of them arrived at Nanny Pamalamadingdong and Granddad Hopalong's home safely after a long flight across the ocean. Nanny P and Granddad H live in the countryside in a little town called Chuckey. It is quieter than in England as the houses are further apart from one another.

Nan explained that Mum is Mom here and Nan or Grandma is Mamaw and Granddad is Papaw.

2.

After resting, Nanny P took the grandchildren to meet her neighbor Steve. He opened his door and said, "Hi y'all. Come on inside and meet my critters." He told them that his German shepherd dog was called Dug. Sophie told him "In England we call that type of dog an Alsatian." "Interesting" replied Steve. "Say hi to Cracker my parrot." "Can he talk?" Zak asked smiling. "Sure can, ask him something," said Steve.

Zak thought for a second and said "Cracker will it be sunny whilst we are here? We are only staying two weeks." Cracker told Zak "They're calling for rain in two days boy." Nigel shouted, "Who calls for rain. Do they stand on the mountain tops and yell for it?" Nanny P told them that was a local expression for "It's going to rain that day." As they were leaving Steve's, Sophie noticed the post person arrive and place the post in the box at the bottom of Steve's driveway. "Oh" she said, "that's neat. Our post goes in our door back home." Nan told her that the post is called the mail and there is a box for the newspaper at the end of the driveway.

"Wow" said Nigel, "so many things are different here Nan." "There is so much more, believe me" she answered.

3.

The next day Nanny asked the grandchildren who would like to taste a typical Tennessee breakfast. "Me,me,me" said all three kids. "Come on then, let's go and eat at Aunt Bessie's restaurant," she said.

On arrival there, they sat and had sausage, biscuit and gravy and something called grits! Nan asked all of them how it was? Zak and Nigel replied, "It's kind of different to English breakfast, toast and boiled egg or fried egg, bacon and sausage." Sophie turned her nose in the air and stated "Gravy is for dinner isn't it Mum?" Alice replied "It's good that we are all different and you ate it didn't you? Be grateful my girl!"

4.

After they had eaten, Nan took them to the grocery store in the car. "Ok you guys," she said. "A trolley is called a buggy or cart here. Zak and Nigel go get me one please." They entered the store and Nan told them to go and get some milk. "Where is it Nan?" they said. "Go and listen for the cow mooing sound and you will know." All three ran around the store as it appeared so big looking for a cow but could only hear the sound as they got nearer the milk and saw the biggest cow statue they had ever seen before. They were giggling when they returned. "That's so neat, even if it is only a recording," said Sophie. "You got us fooled Nan we really thought there was a real cow there," she said still laughing with the boys.

5.

"Now we need to get some fresh vegetables," Nan told them.

As they were standing by the lettuces and greens a loud clap of thunder was heard followed by lightning, and water like rain began spraying on the vegetables! "Oh my gosh" said Susan and Alice and the kids looked startled! "This is so exciting Nan, it beats shopping in England any day" said Nigel. Suddenly, Zak saw a sign that said, Layaway. "What does that mean, Nan?" he asked. Nan explained that you can purchase an item such as a TV or computer or a bike and it gets put in Layaway until you have paid for it in full or you want it left there to collect later when you choose, like for someone's birthday present. "Oh my, Americans think of everything" he answered. As they were checking out the lady on the checkout asked the kids "Are y'all peachy today guys?" "Yeees" they answered quietly and a little hesitant. Nan told her they were from England. The lady at the checkout then told them "Enjoy your trip and come back and see uns soon."

6.

All the family headed on home to see Granddad H and told him all about their experience. He had just come in from feeding the ducks and chickens. "That cockerel is huge Granddad" said Zak! "Yes, he is. His name is Joey and they call them roosters not cockerels here Zak," replied Granddad.

7.

Most evenings were spent on the front porch drinking iced sweet tea and sodas. Granddad explained that sodas are pop and chips are crisps, suckers are lollipops and cookies are biscuits! "We really don't speak the same do we?" he said.

8.

Sometimes the evenings were spent on the back porch in the rockers listening in amazement to the sound of the cicadas known locally as "katydids." These creatures are green like crickets and they could be heard like a buzzing orchestra in the heat of summer. Nan told them, that is their love call to each other. "Listen," she said, "They start slowly and build up to a crescendo and then start again." "There are a lot of "mozzies" here" said Nigel, slapping one of them on his arm. "Yes" replied Granddad. "The locals here call them "skeeters."

9.

Zak and Nigel spent most of the early evening time collecting lightning bugs in nets and placing them in jars. The insect's bodies shimmered with lights darting swiftly through the air in the darkness. Both boys loved doing this with a local boy in the neighborhood.

10.

The kids talked about the different critters like skunks (smelly things!), raccoon's, possums, coyotes, bears and mountain lions. There are snakes, black ones and rattlesnakes. "COOL! Do they have hedgehogs Granddad?" asked Sophie. "No, I don't think so" he answered. "Even the robins and the birds are different and bigger than ours," she said. Granddad told them that there are Blue Jays, Blue Birds, Woodpeckers and the Cardinals. The female Cardinal is brown and the male is red, "The Mockingbird is the native bird of the State of Tennessee," he told them. They were so fascinated to see such tiny birds as the hummingbirds coming so close to drink the sweet water on Nan's outside deck porch. Again, Granddad explained the brown colored ones are the female and the green/ red ones are the males. Alice and Susan found them fascinating but at the same time a little vicious to one another fighting for the nectar!

11.

At the end of the first week, the family took a trip to Dollywood. On the way there, they noticed they were driving on the right side of the road on the Motorway. "No this is known as an Interstate over here but it's similar," said Granddad. "The main road in called the highway and have you noticed the 4 ways" said Susan "when we have been travelling around in the car kids?" "Who has right of way," Zak and Sophie asked?" "The first driver to arrive and then the next and so on in turn," answered Nan.

"Did you know that you can turn right on a red light here if there is nothing coming?" "Wow really" said all the kids, "You are not allowed to turn left on a red light in England it's breaking the law," Sophie spoke with a loud tone of voice.

12.

Dollywood is a theme park owned by the famous Dolly Parton, a country and western singer. The kids enjoyed all the rides and the shows and music and had pictures taken to keep of their trip. Tennessee is the homeland of Music and especially Country and Western and Blue Grass. They do a lot of clogging to the Blue Grass music and fiddles and dulcimers and various string instruments are played to the music. Alice and Susan commented that they would remember their visit to Dollywood for a long time to come. It really was an entertaining day for all.

13.

Nan had a swimming pool in the backyard and a trampoline and a slip slide and the weather was good most days.

On several occasions a young neighbor's boy called Jeff, who was 10 came over to play. He told Sophie, Zak and Nigel that school gets out at the end of May through August. "That's a long break," said Nigel. "We finish school in mid- July through second week in September and get two weeks at Christmas and Easter. We also get spring break and fall break and not as long at Christmas and Easter time here" Jeff answered. "How do you get to school Jeff?" asked Zak. "I catch the school bus with some other kids in this neighborhood. I stand at the bottom of the driveway and wait for it. It brings me home too. Do you know that the driver puts a stop sign out on the side of the bus when he drops each kid off and traffic has to stop in both directions for safety to protect the kids." "Cool" said Nigel. "Our Mums take us to school in the car and even though it's not far it takes forever as the roads are narrower back home and there seems to be a lot more traffic on the roads. Nigel continued to ask Jeff if he wore a uniform." "No just our normal gear" replied Jeff.

14.

Changing the subject as he began to get bored with school questions, he asked the boys "Do you play soccer boys I love to and it's really a game you guys play a lot of in England right?" It's football to us and yes we do especially me" answered Nigel. "I play for Vale Juniors in our county of Cheshire. I play cricket too and rugby, which is kind of similar to your football here, I think? Not totally sure though? he said touching his finger to his lips. "We play basketball and volleyball and a game called rounders, which I guess is similar to baseball here, but I'm not too sure of the rules for baseball?" Sophie said. "Y'all talk like goofballs," said Jeff as they got along "but I can understand y'all, I guess" laughing at them. All the kids enjoyed each other's company and different lingo.

15.

Alice and Susan commented to their Mum and Dad it was good for the kids and themselves to listen to the different terms here in Tennessee as opposed to England. "They will all learn from one another the different words for the same thing, a real learning experience," Susan told Alice, Mum and Dad. "We are too", replied Alice with a smile on her face. She and Susan hooted with laughter at Jeff when he came in saying that Zak was running his mouth at him and his sister and cousin! They both guessed he meant Zak was being cheeky or impudent. Nan told them they were right.

"Running your mouth is so great a term for being cheeky," said both girls. "We can use that one when we get home," said Susan and they laughed cheerfully together.

16.

Towards the end of the two week vacation (called a fortnight - meaning 14 nights in English) the whole family visited the town of Greeneville to take in some history. They visited David Crockett Park near Chuckey and the town of Greeneville where Andrew Johnson who had been the 11th President of the USA was born and saw the museum in memory of him.

17.

They also visited Cherokee and saw an American Native Indian dressed in his colorful tribal clothing. The kids loved his headdress.

18.

Granddad asked the grandkids one evening what they had enjoyed the most out of their visit to Chuckey. Sophie answered she had loved the differences with the mailboxes and having her picture taken with the Native Indian. "I shall have so much to tell them at school when I get back, won't I Granddad" she told him. Zak had loved his time collecting the lightning bugs and playing with Jeff and hoped they had made a new friend? Granddad suggested they write to Jeff and vice versa.

Nigel had noticed the blowing men outside the car dealerships and loved them, as he had never seen them back home.

19.

Granddad told all the kids that when he went to the Doctors one time he was asked to put on a gown by the nurse and just to crack the door when he was ready.

All three grandkids laughed as they asked him did he do it? "Did you beat the door down Granddad?" asked Nigel. "No," he laughed and told them that it meant leave the door ajar or open. "It appears I have had to learn a different language living here and it's been fun." Another time I was undoing a screw and was told by this man that they say lefty loosy and righty tighty when doing that. "That's so neat," said Zak and it makes so much sense. "I'm fixin to" means I'm about to leave to go to the shops, leave the house or do some mowing or just go about my business he said.

20.

"All good visits, holidays or vacations, whatever we call them have to come to an end," said Nanny on the last evening sadly. "Your Dad's will have missed you all in England and be happy to have you home again. We shall miss all of you but I know we shall have you come over again very soon. The whole world seems easier to travel around than it was when I was your age kids," she told them sighing.

21.

The last night was spent around a bonfire eating barbecue, known locally as a cookout, watching the sunset whilst dilly dallying or lollygagging as they say here in Chuckey. Lots of fun, laughter and chitter - chattering echoed from the whole family. "We are really going to miss this place Mum and Dad and you both especially," said Susan and Alice. They all embraced in a huge hug!

22.

Saying goodbye at the airport to all of them was hard and a few tears shed — but everyone knew they would return to sweet Tennessee!

Good-bye Tennessee
It's been fun to know you
What we take away with us
Is memories of Southern lingo –
The differences in our language
For the same things
Of sun and sounds and mountain
views
Birds, critters, good viddles and
friends

We may be 3,000 miles away but
In spirit we are near
We will return to you one day
Until then... let's shout it out
REAL LOUD AND CLEAR

Ta, ta, bye bye, cheerio, chin chin
Catch you later, Come see uns!
They are expressions that mean
the same
No matter where you come from
C' ya uns later!

Author BIO:

Pamalamadingdong is my name

I have been a teacher in College in the UK for many years. I moved to Tennessee to retire. NO WAY!

I have owned a Professional Cleaning Company for 11 years now.

I am a mother of two daughters a step son, have 6 grandchildren and 2 great grandchildren, a boy and a girl. I have also fostered 8 teenagers here in Tennessee and am a 'recycled teenager' myself, living life to the full.

You can check on my website:
www.pamyoungauthors.com

About the Illustrator:

Brynne-Elisabeth C. Carlisle was born in Southern Romania and was adopted at the age of 3, coming to America for a second chance in life.

She graduated from East Tennessee State University with a Bachelor of Fine Arts in graphic design/illustration. Brynne is an award winning illustrator and was published in the Creative Quarterly #52. She is a part of ETSU's art collection as one of her narrative illustrations has been selected.

Creative and witty, Brynne loves her two kitties, Bonnie and Boo and adores nature and dancing.

Chocolate chip cookies are her favorite desserts to eat!

You can check on my website:
https://brynnecarlisle7.wixsite.com/mysite